AUTHOR DEDICATION

For Talya Sokoll

D0996948

Reycraft Books
55 Fifth Avenue
New York, NY 10003
Reycraftbooks.com

Reycraft Books is a trade imprint and trademark of Newmark Learning, LLC.

Educators and Librarians: Our books may be purchased in bulk for promotional, educational, or business use. Please contact sales@reycraftbooks.com.

Library of Congress Control Number: 2020900886

ISBN: 978-1-4788-6863-7

Illustration credit: Luciano Lozano

Photograph credits: Jacket (front, texture), Jacket (back), Cover (texture), Title Page (red texture), Back Cover (background) © crabgarden/Shutterstock; Pages i, ii, iii, 32–35 (background) © mattponchik/Shutterstock; Page 32 (author photo) courtesy of Charles Ludeke.

Printed in Guangzhou, China
4401/0120/CA22000032
10 9 8 7 6 5 4 3 2 1

First Edition Hardcover published by Reycraft Books, 2020

Reycraft Books and Newmark Learning, LLC. support diversity and the First Amendment, and celebrate the right to read.

Max

on the Farm

BY KYLE LUKOFF · ILLUSTRATED BY LUCIANO LOZANO

Chapter 1

My friend Teresa likes to get dirty.

REALLY dirty.

We have worm-digging contests.

We roll down hills.

I bury her in the sandbox, and then she buries me.

I don't like getting into trouble.

Sometimes it happens.

But it only happens when I play with Teresa.

There was the time we got our Frisbee stuck on the roof.

And the time we made an awful cake

out of EVERYTHING in the kitchen.

And the time we got trapped
under Teresa's porch.

Teresa doesn't care about getting in trouble.
She says it's part of having fun.

But we won't have time to get in trouble today.
Or tomorrow.

Our class is going on a field trip to a real farm!
We will sleep in something called a hayloft. We will feed goats.
And maybe ride horses. I want to milk a cow.
Farms sound like very busy places.

When we get there, the farmer says to follow him to the hayloft.

I don't even know what a hayloft is.
We climb up a shaky ladder.

I guess a hayloft is a big room on top of a barn.

The farmer says that girls sleep on one side
and boys on the other.
He points me to the girl side.
The teacher pulls him aside to explain.

I lay my sleeping bag next to Steven's.
Teresa waves at me from the girl side.

Chapter 2

There is so much work to do on a farm.

I wonder if farmer kids have time to get in trouble.

We learn how a plow works.

We learn what a silo is.

We learn how much poop cows make in a day. (A lot!)

The farmer says that milking cows is done by machines now.
So we don't learn how to do that.

But not all the work is hard.

We play with baby chicks.
They jump and peep and are softer than kittens.

We ride horses.

I was scared, but my horse seemed to know that and walked slowly.

The farmer tells us there are baby piglets.

But they are inside the pigpen.

Their mama doesn't want to show them off.

At dinner we eat and eat and eat.
Farmwork makes you hungry.
And the food is delicious.

"I made it myself," says the farmer's son.

"The corn is so sweet!" says Teresa.

"I picked it myself!" says the farmer's wife.

Everyone likes the cookies we got for dessert.

Then we learn how to square dance.

They split the dance into a boys' side and a girls' side.

The square dance teacher thought I should be on the girls' side.

I sneak over to the boys' side.

All the kids in my class know I belong there.

Square dancing is NOT my favorite.

Then it is bedtime. It is too dark to see outside.

We climb up the ladder to the hayloft.

We change into our pajamas and crawl into our sleeping bags.

We turn off our flashlights. Soon everyone is asleep.

16

Everyone **EXCEPT** me and Teresa.

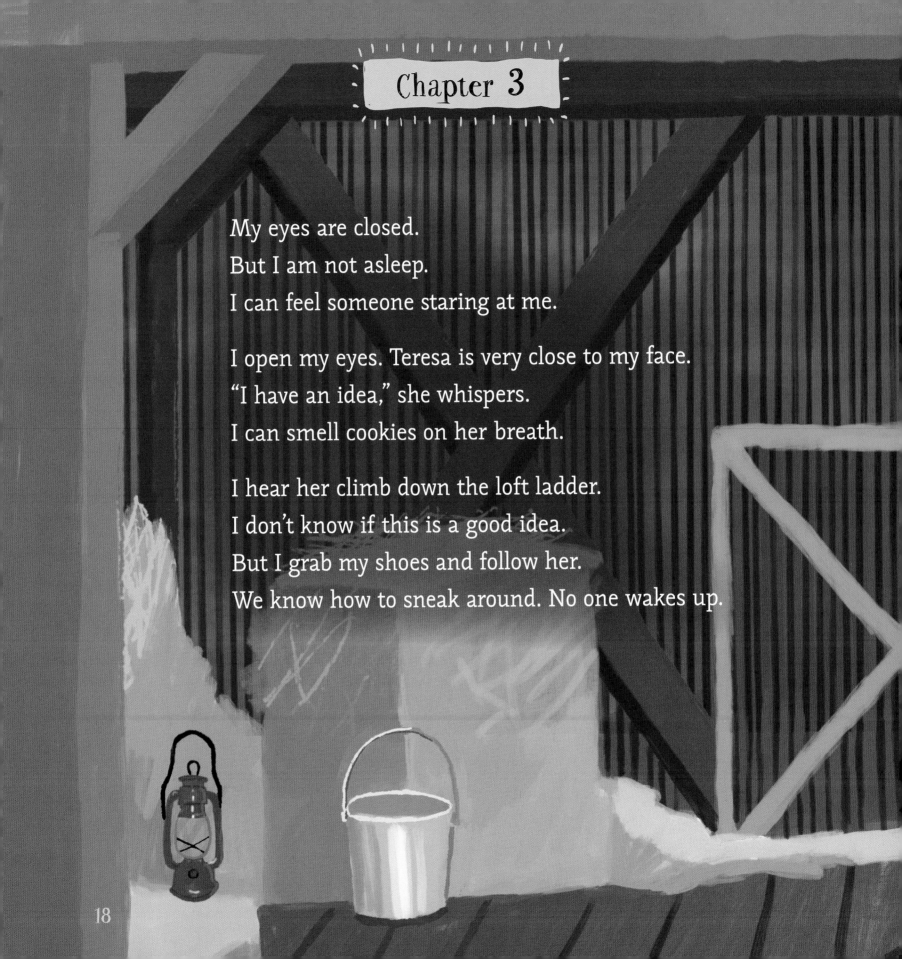

Chapter 3

My eyes are closed.

But I am not asleep.

I can feel someone staring at me.

I open my eyes. Teresa is very close to my face.

"I have an idea," she whispers.

I can smell cookies on her breath.

I hear her climb down the loft ladder.

I don't know if this is a good idea.

But I grab my shoes and follow her.

We know how to sneak around. No one wakes up.

19

We tiptoe out of the barn and turn on our flashlights.
"I want to see the baby pigs," she says.
"Let's go into the pigpen. We can pet them."

I have seen pictures of piglets. They are very cute.
I don't know if this is a good idea.
But Teresa doesn't seem worried.

We sneak over to the pigpen.
We climb over the fence
and squish across the pen.
The mud is sticky and stinky.
I hope that it's only mud.

The baby pigs are sleeping
next to their mama.
The mama pig is huge.
And ugly.

The baby pigs are tiny. And so cute.
Maybe this was a good idea.
Teresa reaches out her hand.
She pats one of the baby pigs.
It snorts, just a little.

That little snort wakes up the mama pig.

It turns out pigs can be very loud.

And mama pigs don't like it when kids try to touch their babies.

24

The mama pig chases us out of the pigpen. We run toward the fence.
I trip and fall into the mud. Teresa tries to pull me up.
She falls too. We see flashlights coming from the farmhouse.
Our flashlights are gone. Will we get into trouble?

Chapter 4

We climb back over the fence.
The farmer runs over to the pigpen
to see what's wrong.

He doesn't see us.
We hide behind a truck.
Then we run back to the hayloft.

The pigs must have woken up our class.
Everyone is standing outside the barn.
But only the teacher has a flashlight.
No one sees us sneak into the barn
and back up into the hayloft.

We take off our muddy pajamas,
put on our normal clothes,
and crawl into our sleeping bags.
Soon everyone goes back to bed.
No one asks where we were.
Maybe no one noticed we were gone.

We didn't get to play with the piglets. But we didn't get into trouble.
I hope my mom won't ask why my pajamas are filthy and smelly.

If she does, I'll just say that Teresa and I went on an adventure. Mom is used to that.

Kyle Lukoff has worked at the intersection of books and people for over half his life, first as a bookseller, then as a school librarian, and now as a writer. He is transgender, like Max, and lives in a small Brooklyn apartment with six overflowing bookshelves.

Luciano Lozano was born the same year Man traveled to the Moon. That may be the reason why he has traveled a lot since childhood. When not traveling he lives in Barcelona. His illustrations reflect his strong sense of color and texture, as well as his subtle sense of humor.